Remember the Ladies

BY CALLISTA GINGRICH

ILLUSTRATED BY SUSAN ARCIERO

★ ★ ★ ★ ★ Acknowledgments ★ ★ ★ ★ ★

Thank you to the incredible people who have made this book possible.

I especially want to thank Susan Arciero, whose outstanding illustrations have once again brought Ellis the Elephant to life.

The team at Regnery Kids has made writing *Remember the Ladies* a real pleasure. Thanks to Marji Ross and Cheryl Barnes for their insightful and creative contributions. Regnery has been remarkable in turning this book into a reality.

My sincere gratitude goes to our staff at Gingrich Productions, including Bess Kelly, Christina Maruna, Woody Hales, Audrey Bird, John Hines, Louie Brogdon, and Kristen Wuerl. Their support has been invaluable.

Finally, I'd like to thank my husband, Newt. His enthusiasm for the Ellis the Elephant series has been my source of inspiration.

Regnery Kids™ is a trademark of Salem Communications Holding Corporation;
Regnery® is a registered trademark of Salem Communications Holding Corporation

Cataloging-in-Publication data on file with the Library of Congress

ISBN 978-1-62157-480-4
e-book ISBN 978-1-62157-574-0

Published in the United States by
Regnery Kids
An imprint of Regnery Publishing
A Division of Salem Media Group
300 New Jersey Ave NW
Washington, DC 20001
www.RegneryKids.com

Manufactured in the United States of America

10 9 8 7 6 5 4 3 2 1

Books are available in quantity for promotional or premium use.
For information on discounts and terms, please visit our website: www.Regnery.com.

Distributed to the trade by
Perseus Distribution
www.perseusdistribution.com

Dedicated to the first ladies
of the United States of America.

Ellis the Elephant knew every president's tale,
how each led America and helped it prevail.
But Ellis knew there was more to their success—
the brilliant first ladies with whom they were blessed.

The first ladies were strong—a diverse group of wives,
who each on their own lived remarkable lives.
Through good times and bad, they willingly served,
so liberty and freedom would be preserved.

Martha Washington was quite famous in her day.
Her example showed other first ladies the way.
After her husband, George, won the Revolution,
together they made many contributions.

The first lady's role was Martha's invention.
She approached her work with care and attention.
Her dignity and grace were widely admired.
The "Mother of our Country" left a nation inspired.

Abigail Adams had her husband's respect.
She gave frequent advice that was often direct.
As our Founders created the nation anew,
she advised John: "Remember the ladies" too!

She asked him to listen to women's voices—
so they'd be included in major choices.
As first lady, Abigail lived where no one had been—
at the White House, where she was the first to move in.

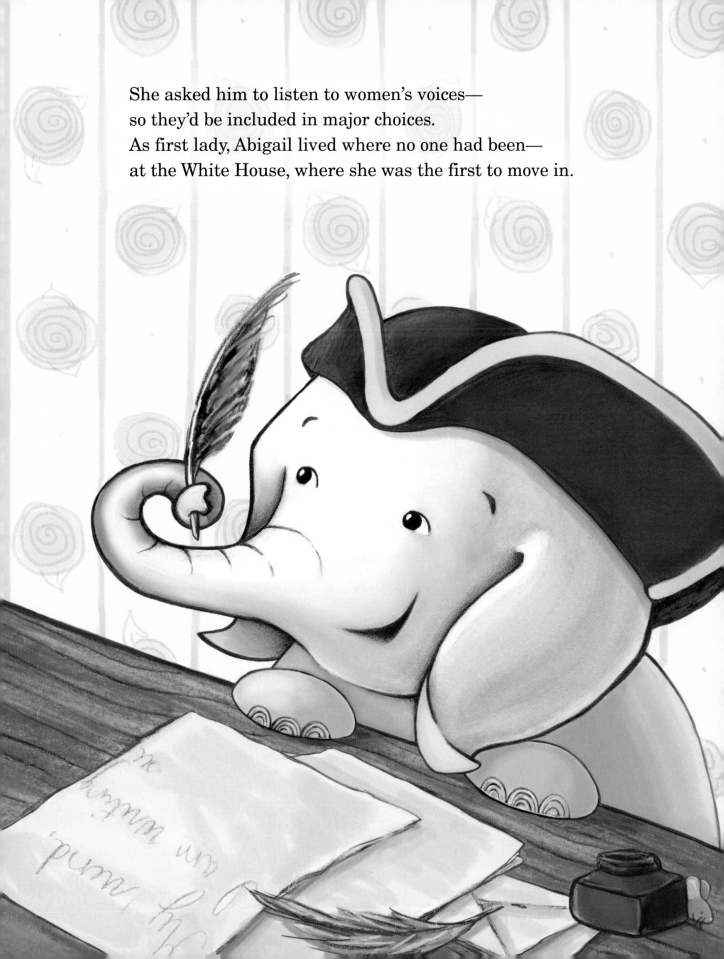

Dolley Madison was known for beauty and charm,
but while in the White House, she had cause for alarm.
As the British invaded America once more,
the Madisons presided over a nation at war.

In Washington the British set the White House ablaze,
and Dolley made the narrowest of great getaways!
She saved a national treasure in that close call
and rescued Washington's portrait right off the wall!

Ellis learned next about Abigail Fillmore,
a friendly first lady who many adored.
Like Ellis, Abigail was an avid reader,
and she shared her love as a national leader.

Abigail added a library to the White House,
a lasting contribution from Millard Fillmore's spouse.
Smart and inquisitive, this former teacher
selected books for the library to feature.

Abe Lincoln was president throughout the Civil War.
And his wife, Mary Todd, knew what the fight was for.
She wished to end slavery with full emancipation—
and encouraged her husband to make a proclamation.

Mary tended to troops who were hurt in the fight,
lifting their spirits for a cause that was right.
She worked hard to keep the U.S. Army supplied,
so the Union could win and heal the nation's divide.

Being first lady was Nellie Taft's major goal,
and she quickly grew into her new leading role.
As a partner and hostess, she was first class—
as was her cow on the White House grass!

Nellie left her mark on our capital city,
with a lasting gift that made it so pretty.
As first lady she planted many cherry trees,
that still bloom brightly and blow in the breeze.

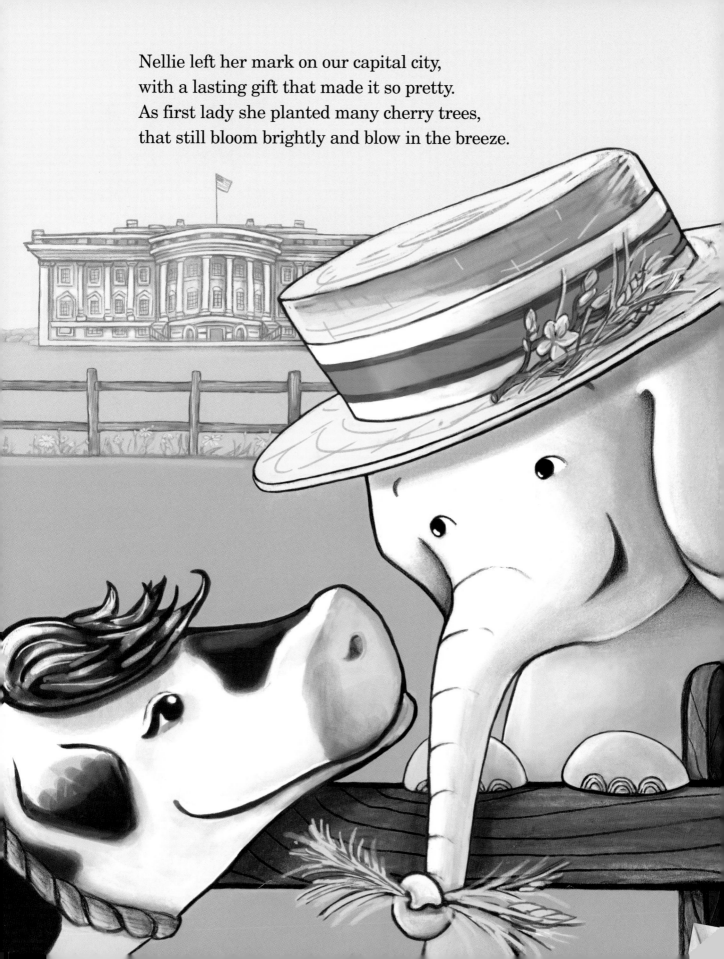

No woman has ever held our nation's top post,
but Ellis learned that Edith Wilson came close.
She ably assisted when her husband fell ill,
so Woodrow Wilson could be president still.

Edith was a woman with courage and brains,
who cared for her husband and then took the reins.
With caution and wisdom, she fulfilled his commands—
the people unaware they were safe in her hands.

Eleanor Roosevelt was remarkable too—
a leading first lady with her own point of view.
She made human rights and equality her mission—
and the first lady's job a full-time position.

In meetings with the nation's female reporters,
she answered questions from foes and supporters.
When Ellis learned of all that Eleanor had done,
he thought she should've made a presidential run!

Jackie Kennedy was an instant sensation.
With glamour and grace, she charmed the whole nation.
In an era of hope, some people thought,
the Kennedys had become the new Camelot.

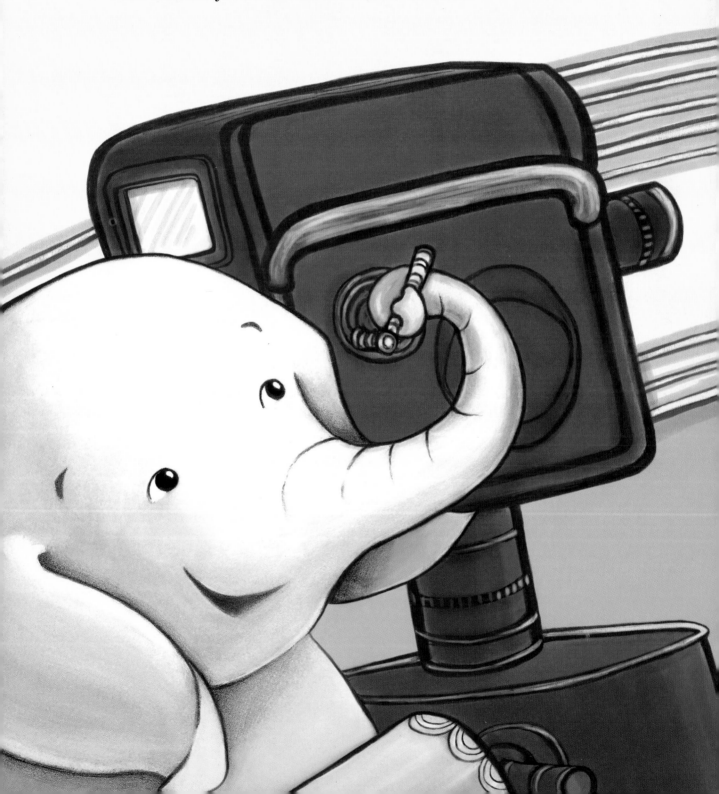

Jackie soon added to this sense of allure
when she took Americans on a special tour.
For the very first time, everyone could see,
the beauty of the White House on national TV!

Lady Bird Johnson was rather distressed
that America's roadsides weren't looking their best.
She worked hard to make sure they didn't become
littered with trash, all dirty and glum!

Congress decided to give Lady Bird the power
to line the highways with beautiful flowers.
Ellis thought Americans could take great pride
in a country that was restored and beautified.

Nancy Reagan left her life as a Hollywood star
for a stage with a brighter spotlight by far.
As a wife, she had Ronald's listening ear
and encouraged him in his elected career.

While first lady, Nancy launched a major campaign
to put an end to a problem that caused much pain.
She wanted drug-free schools where children could grow
and urged young Americans to "Just Say No!"

Laura Bush was a daughter of the Lone Star State.
A charming first lady, her impact was great.
This former schoolteacher was eager to lead
a movement to teach every student to read.

Laura travelled the country visiting kids in school
and helped them to see that books could be cool!
Admiring her efforts, Ellis could tell
that he and Laura would get along well.

Michelle Obama made great historic gains,
asking children to stretch their muscles and brains.
She challenged them to enjoy daily exercise
and led by example to their pleasant surprise.

Michelle urged young people to get up and move
and encouraged them all to get into the groove.
Ellis was soft, and he had to admit
that with Michelle's advice, he could be more fit!

Ellis thought about the first ladies he had met,
and the others he had not learned about yet.
All had their own special talents and traits
that they used to make the United States great.

They comforted our nation in moments of need
and offered leadership to help America succeed.
Ellis was grateful for what the first ladies had done,
and now understood: We should remember each one!

★ ★ ★ ★ ★ Resources ★ ★ ★ ★ ★

Martha Washington (1789–1797)

Martha Washington pioneered and defined the role of first lady as a gracious hostess and supportive spouse. Many of the standards and traditions set by Martha have been upheld by first ladies for more than two centuries. She and President George Washington lived in New York during his presidency. They later returned to their estate, Mount Vernon, in Virginia.

Abigail Adams (1797–1801)

Abigail and John Adams were the first family to live in the White House—although at the time it was called the Executive Mansion. Abigail was vocal about her political views and served as John's closest advisor. When he was away, she regularly wrote him letters updating him on politics and the news of the day. Famously, she urged him to "remember the ladies" as he drafted the Declaration of Independence.

Martha Jefferson (died 1782)

Martha Jefferson never actually served as first lady. She died in 1782, nearly twenty years before her husband, Thomas Jefferson, became president.

Thomas never remarried and managed many of the social affairs in the White House on his own, although he occasionally relied on Dolley Madison, the wife of future president James Madison, to help with events. Thomas's daughter, Patsy, also served as White House hostess for a short time.

Dolley Madison (1809–1817)

Dolley Madison was the wife of the "Father of the Constitution," James Madison. She fully embraced the social obligations of the first lady and regularly held large parties at the White House for people from differing political and social backgrounds. Dolley was also first lady during the first wartime presidency. When the British burned the White House during the War of 1812, she courageously saved a famous portrait of George Washington from the fire. After serving as first lady, Dolley influenced Washington social life for decades.

Elizabeth Monroe (1817–1825)

Elizabeth Monroe was the wife of James Monroe. Elizabeth shunned the social responsibilities associated with the role of first lady. While she was criticized for breaking tradition, her example allowed future first ladies to chart their own courses. It's widely believed that Elizabeth lived with epilepsy, a disease which was stigmatized at the time.

Louisa Adams (1825–1829)

Louisa Adams met and married John Quincy Adams when he served as a diplomat in England. When Louisa became first lady, she hosted numerous parties at the White House to support her husband. She frequently played harp and piano to entertain guests.

★ ★ ★ ★ ★ Resources ★ ★ ★ ★ ★

Rachel Jackson (died 1828)

Like Martha Jefferson, Rachel Jackson never served as first lady. She died of a heart attack shortly after her husband, Andrew Jackson, was elected president. In her honor, Andrew planted a magnolia tree outside of the White House. Rachel's niece, Emily Donelson, fulfilled the role of hostess during Andrew Jackson's presidency.

Hannah Van Buren (died 1819)

Hannah Van Buren also died nearly two decades before her husband became president. Very little is known about Hannah's life. Her husband, Martin Van Buren, did not even mention her in his autobiography. After Martin took office, his daughter-in-law, Angelica Van Buren, served as the White House hostess. Angelica threw many extravagant parties and was criticized for having European taste.

Anna Harrison (1841)

Anna Harrison's time as first lady was short because her husband, William Henry Harrison, died from pneumonia thirty-two days after assuming office. At the time, Anna was sixty-five and had the distinction of being the nation's oldest first lady. Anna was also the grandmother of another president, Benjamin Harrison, who was the nation's twenty-third commander in chief.

Letitia Tyler (1841–1842)

Letitia Tyler served as first lady to her husband, John Tyler, for only two years before she died following a long illness related to a stroke. She was the first presidential spouse to die in the White House. Until he remarried, John relied on their daughter-in-law, Priscilla Tyler, to serve as White House hostess. Priscilla relied heavily on the advice of renowned socialite and former first lady Dolley Madison in managing social affairs.

Julia Tyler (1844–1845)

Julia Tyler became first lady after marrying President John Tyler during the second half of his presidency. Julia immediately assumed social duties and hosted opulent White House parties. Just like past first ladies, Julia used social events to influence legislation—throwing a two-thousand-person party to support the annexation of Texas in 1845.

Sarah Polk (1845–1849)

Sarah Polk was a behind-the-scenes political advisor for her husband, President James Polk. She eschewed many of the social duties of first lady and instead helped James write speeches and research legislation. The two even shared an office in the White House. At formal dinners, Sarah would often discuss politics with men instead of socializing with women and would sometimes get so immersed in conversation that she would forget to eat.

Margaret "Peggy" Taylor (1849–1850)

Peggy Taylor opposed her husband, Zachary Taylor's election as president, and she refused to serve as White House hostess. Instead, their twenty-two-year-old daughter, Betty Taylor, assumed social duties. Peggy would occasionally join Zachary for official dinners. Her time in the White House was brief, as Zachary died after only sixteen months in office.

★ ★ ★ ★ ★ Resources ★ ★ ★ ★ ★

Abigail Fillmore (1850–1853)

Abigail Fillmore's life exemplified the American dream. She was born to a poor family in New York, became a school teacher, and later married Millard Fillmore, who became the thirteenth president of the United States. Her biggest contribution as first lady was creating the first White House library, which she meticulously curated. Her background in education, along with her love of learning, made her an indispensable advisor to Millard.

Jane Pierce (1853–1857)

Jane Pierce disapproved of politics and reportedly prayed that her husband, Franklin Pierce, would not become president. Shortly after Franklin was elected, the Pierces' young son, Bennie, tragically died in a train accident. Jane's sadness prevented her from performing the first lady's duties, and friends took the responsibility in her stead.

Harriet Lane Johnston (1857–1861)

President James Buchanan was the first and only bachelor president. Upon taking office, he relied on his niece, Harriet Johnston, to serve as first lady and manage social affairs. To keep peace, Harriet enforced a rule that guests were not allowed to discuss politics at White House parties.

Mary Todd Lincoln (1861–1865)

Mary Todd Lincoln was greatly affected by the Civil War, and she spent much of her time as first lady helping injured Union soldiers at hospitals. Like her husband, Abraham Lincoln, Mary was devoted to ending slavery and promoting the rights of all Americans. She encouraged President Lincoln to issue the Emancipation Proclamation on January 1, 1863.

Eliza Johnson (1865–1869)

Eliza Johnson was suffering from tuberculosis when her husband, Andrew Johnson, became president following the tragic assassination of President Lincoln. Consequently, their daughter Martha Johnson served as the White House hostess. Eliza did, however, advise Andrew on policy decisions.

Julia Grant (1869–1877)

When her husband, Ulysses Grant, became president after leading the Union Army to victory in the Civil War, Julia Grant fully embraced the role of first lady. She became famous for holding glamorous dinners—some of which included twenty-nine courses. While previous first ladies had been criticized for their extravagance, Julia's flashy style gave comfort and pride to a country recovering from war. After her time as first lady, Julia advocated for women's rights and supported the suffrage movement.

Lucy Hayes (1877–1881)

Lucy Hayes was a stark contrast to Julia Grant. After Lucy's husband, Rutherford B. Hayes, became president, formal dinners virtually ceased at the White House. Lucy, who was a conservative woman and the first presidential spouse to graduate from college, held informal gatherings in the evenings instead. She travelled the nation and supported Civil War orphans. Lucy also redecorated and modernized the presidential mansion and was responsible for bringing the first telephone into the White House.

★ ★ ★ ★ ★ Resources ★ ★ ★ ★ ★

Lucretia "Crete" Garfield (1881)

Crete Garfield was not first lady for long, as her husband, James Garfield, was shot and killed only months after taking the oath of office. During her time in the White House, Crete was recovering from malaria and stayed out of public life. She allowed only one photograph to be taken of her as first lady.

Ellen "Nell" Arthur (died 1880)

President Chester Arthur did not have an official first lady. His wife, Nell, died of pneumonia twenty months before he took office. Chester's youngest sister, Mary Arthur McElroy, served as White House hostess during his administration. Chester mourned Nell's death for most of his presidency.

Frances Cleveland (1886–1889, 1893–1897)

Frances Cleveland was the only first lady to move in and out of the White House twice after her husband, Grover Cleveland, was elected to non-consecutive terms. At twenty-one, Frances was the youngest first lady. She was both the first person to marry a president in the White House and the first to give birth there. Frances fully performed all social and advisory duties of the first lady and advocated for women's education.

Caroline "Carrie" Harrison (1889–1892)

Carrie Harrison was known as the White House's most devout housekeeper. After her husband, Benjamin Harrison, who was the grandson of President William Harrison, took office, Carrie updated the kitchens and bathrooms in the White House. She also brought electric lighting to the White House and started a china collection. Carrie advocated for equal education for women and raised money for Johns Hopkins University School of Medicine, which in turn accepted female students.

Ida McKinley (1897–1901)

Ida McKinley overcame serious illness to carry out her duties as first lady. Despite suffering from what historians believe was epilepsy, Ida would accompany her husband, William McKinley, to all White House social gatherings. Her time as first lady was cut short, however, after William was shot and killed during his second term.

Edith "Edie" Roosevelt (1901–1909)

Edie Roosevelt was the complete opposite of her outgoing, energetic husband Theodore "Teddy" Roosevelt. But despite her private nature, Edie invited musicians to perform at the White House and regularly held social gatherings. She led an effort to recover historical furnishings that had once been in the White House. She was also responsible for building the West Wing offices, which helped make the president's living quarters more private.

Helen "Nellie" Taft (1909–1913)

Nellie Taft was ambitious, politically savvy, and very intelligent. She frequently helped her husband, President Howard Taft, select cabinet members and diplomats. As first lady, Nellie had more than three thousand Japanese cherry trees planted throughout Washington, D.C. She also brought a milk cow to the White House lawn.

★ ★ ★ ★ ★ Resources ★ ★ ★ ★ ★

Ellen Wilson (1913–1914)

Ellen Wilson was the first wife of President Woodrow Wilson. As first lady, she took an interest in improving working conditions for female government employees. She also advocated for improving poor neighborhoods in Washington, D.C. Ellen died of Bright's disease during Woodrow's first term.

Edith Wilson (1915–1921)

Edith Wilson, the second wife of President Woodrow Wilson, faced unique challenges while serving as first lady. After Woodrow suffered a stroke in 1919, Edith became his chief caretaker and liaison to the Congress. Many viewed Edith as the de facto president.

Florence Harding (1921–1923)

Florence Harding was a critical advisor to her husband, President Warren Harding. She helped him write speeches and think through policy decisions. Florence was also instrumental in his election, leading a campaign that appealed to women—who had just gained the right to vote. As first lady, Florence was the first to speak publicly to the press and the first to receive Secret Service protection. Her time as first lady was cut short after Warren died of a blood clot during his term.

Grace Coolidge (1923–1929)

Grace and Calvin Coolidge were something of an odd couple. Grace was lively and outgoing, while Calvin was quiet and reserved. He was often referred to as "Silent Cal." While Grace did not engage in politics, she had a great impact on American culture. In 1931, she was voted one of "America's Twelve Greatest Women."

Lou Hoover (1929–1933)

Lou Hoover was the most well-traveled first lady of her time. Before her husband, President Herbert Hoover, took office, the two had traveled extensively thorough Australia, Japan, Europe, Egypt, and China. Lou spoke seven languages and was the first American woman to earn a geology degree. As first lady, she was a vocal advocate for the rights of women and African Americans. Lou also threw lavish parties at the White House, which were criticized as the country was enduring the Great Depression.

Eleanor Roosevelt (1933–1945)

Eleanor Roosevelt served longer than any other first lady. She was the wife and political partner of Franklin Delano Roosevelt. As first lady, Eleanor promoted civil rights and strongly supported women's rights. Eleanor even held press conferences in the White House exclusively for female journalists. After leaving the White House, she continued public service as a delegate to the United Nations and led the UN Commission on Human Rights.

Elizabeth "Bess" Truman (1945–1953)

Like many before her, Bess Truman did not enjoy the spotlight that came with being first lady. She consequently held very few social gatherings at the White House. Her practicality earned her the respect of Americans. Bess was very engaged in the presidency of her husband, Harry Truman. Together they discussed policy issues and speeches.

Mamie Eisenhower (1953–1961)

Mamie Eisenhower focused entirely on hosting duties while serving in the White House with her husband, President Dwight D. Eisenhower. Her fashion sense, kind demeanor, and willingness to greet tourists earned her the respect and adoration of many Americans. Mamie was famous for her trademark bangs.

Jacqueline "Jackie" Kennedy (1961–1963)

Jackie Kennedy brought youthful style and glamour to the White House. She fully renovated the White House and invited all Americans to see the presidential mansion through a televised tour in 1962. She also returned to the tradition of making the White House a social and cultural center of the nation, inviting popular musicians and artists to perform.

Claudia "Lady Bird" Johnson (1963–1969)

Lady Bird Johnson served as first lady during an extraordinary time in American history. Her husband, Lyndon B. Johnson, led the country after the tragic assassination of John F. Kennedy and signed into law the Civil Rights Act, which Lady Bird fully supported. As first lady, Lady Bird worked to enhance our country through her "Beautify America" campaign. Her advocacy resulted in the Highway Beautification Act of 1965, which limited unsightly advertising and improved the scenery along federal highways.

Thelma "Pat" Nixon (1969–1974)

Pat Nixon is known as the most well-traveled first lady of all time. After her husband, Richard Nixon, was elected, the two traveled to more than eighty countries. Although she was not eager to be first lady, Pat was a diligent hostess and started Christmas and garden tours at the White House, as well as tours for the blind.

Elizabeth "Betty" Ford (1974–1977)

As first lady, Betty Ford was a strong advocate for women's rights and health. Shortly after her husband, Gerald Ford, became president following resignation of President Nixon, Betty was diagnosed with breast cancer. Instead of keeping her illness a secret, Betty started a public campaign to urge women to get regular screenings for the disease. In 1982, she established the Betty Ford Center for Drug and Alcohol Rehabilitation to help those with substance abuse problems.

Eleanor "Rosalynn" Carter (1977–1981)

Rosalynn and Jimmy Carter operated the White House as a team. Rosalynn did almost everything with Jimmy. She routinely attended cabinet meetings and participated in policy discussions. Rosalynn also publicly supported equal rights for women and championed policies to improve mental health care in America.

Nancy Reagan (1981–1989)

Like her husband, Ronald Reagan, Nancy began her career acting. As first lady, Nancy was known for her "Just Say No" campaign that was aimed at teaching children the dangers of drug abuse. After her time as first lady, she became a committed advocate for curing Alzheimer's disease, which afflicted her husband late in life.

Barbara Bush (1989–1993)

Barbara Bush spent most of her time as first lady focusing on literacy, homelessness, and the AIDS epidemic. After her husband, George H. W. Bush, was inaugurated, Barbara started the Barbara Bush

★ ★ ★ ★ ★ Resources ★ ★ ★ ★ ★

Foundation for Family Literacy and advocated for equal rights for minorities and immigrants. Her son, George W. Bush, became president in 2001.

Hillary Clinton (1993–2001)

Hillary Clinton played an active role in policy-making during the administration of her husband, Bill Clinton. Most famously, she led a task force on health care reform. She also championed the rights of women and children worldwide. After serving as first lady, Hillary became a U.S. senator and the first female presidential nominee from a major political party.

Laura Bush (2001–2009)

Laura Bush spent most of her adult life as an educator. When her husband, George W. Bush, became president, she continued her life's work from the White House. As first lady, Laura focused her efforts on promoting literacy and reading programs in schools. Starting in 2001, Laura traveled several times to Afghanistan to support women's rights and education.

Michelle Obama (2009–2017)

Michelle Obama was our nation's first African American first lady. Prior to her husband's election, she had a successful professional career in law, government, academia, and finally as a hospital administrator. After Barack Obama took office, she focused on her "Let's Move!" campaign, which promoted healthy eating and exercise programs to help prevent childhood obesity.

Melania Trump (2017–)

Born in Slovenia, Melania Trump was the first immigrant to become first lady. She officially became a U.S. citizen in 2006. Before coming to the White House, Melania was a fashion model, a philanthropist, and an entrepreneur.